BRIGHT and EARLY BOOKS for BEGINNING Beginners

This Book Belongs to...

© Illus. Dr. Seuss 1957

www.randomhouse.com/kids/

Library of Congress Cataloging-in-Publication Data
Corey, Shana. Babe : oops, pig! / by Shana Corey ; illustrated by Donald Cook ; based on characters created by Dick King-Smith. p. cm. — (Early step into reading)
SUMMARY: Babe the pig gets into mischief when he tries to help out with chores on the farm.
ISBN 0-679-88967-1 (pbk.) — ISBN 0-679-98967-6 (lib. bdg.)
[1. Pigs—Fiction. 2. Farm life—Fiction.] I. Cook, Donald, ill. II. Title. III. Series.
PZ7.C8155Bad 1998 [E]—dc21 97-40800

Printed in the United States of America   10 9 8 7 6 5 4 3 2 1

EARLY STEP INTO READING is a trademark of Random House, Inc.

GROLIER
BOOK CLUB EDITION

BABE
The Sheep Pig™

Oops, Pig!

By Shana Corey

Illustrated by Donald Cook

Based on characters created by Dick King-Smith

Random House 🏠 New York

The sun comes up.
"Quack-a-doodle-doo!"
shouts the duck.

Babe is still asleep.

Wake up, sleepyhead!

Time for breakfast!

Pancakes for the farmer.

Hay for the horses.

Feed for the chickens.

And slop for Babe!

Time for chores.

Gather the eggs, Babe.

Milk the cow, Babe.

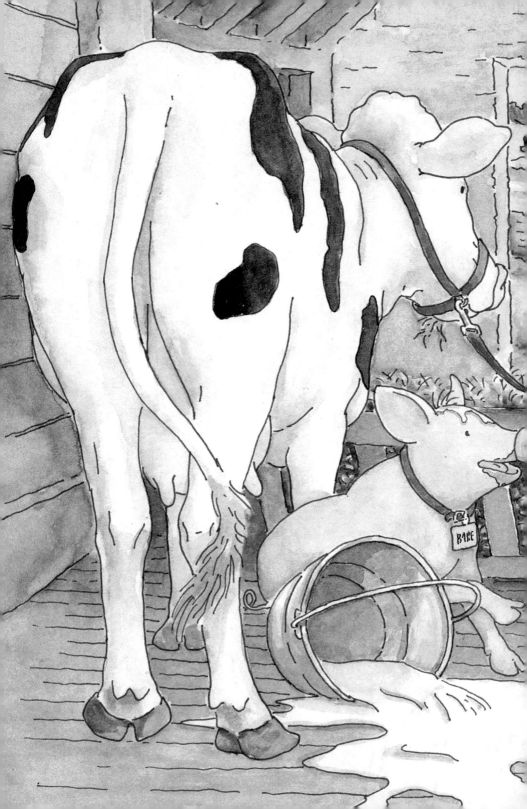

Weed the garden, Babe.

Oh, dear!

"Babe! What a mess
you have made!"

Babe wants to help.

What can he do?

Babe can herd sheep!

"Good job, Pig,"

says the farmer.